It was a **special day**.
The Railway Inspector was
coming to Sodor.

"Thomas, you should be shunting
coal trucks when the Inspector comes,"
said The Fat Controller. "He wants to
see **busy engines**."

Thomas went to find more engines to help shunt trucks.

He puffed to Maron Station. Percy was waiting for the mail.

"Hello, Percy," peeped Thomas. "Will you come and shunt coal trucks with me? The Inspector wants to see **busy engines!**"

Percy was meant to deliver the mail, but he wanted to help Thomas. Percy was uncoupled, and away he *whooshed*.

When the Inspector arrived at Maron Station, Percy wasn't there! The Inspector was **not** very pleased.

Thomas huffed to
the Quarry, where Mavis
was waiting to pull some slate trucks.

"Will you come and shunt coal trucks?"
peeped Thomas. "The Inspector
wants to see **busy engines!**"

Mavis had a lot to do, but she decided
to help Thomas, too.

When the Inspector arrived at the Quarry, Mavis wasn't there.

The Inspector was **not** pleased at all!

Thomas chuffed cheerily back to the Docks.

Percy and Mavis had already shunted a **long** line of coal trucks. The Inspector would be pleased!

Then Thomas heard Gordon's whistle **peep** as he brought the Inspector to the Docks.

"We must look busy!" wheeshed Thomas.

So Percy **shoved** … and Mavis **shunted** … and the coal trucks **biffed** and **bashed** together!

Coal dust flew down Gordon's funnel and made him **splutter** and cough.

The Fat Controller was **cross**. "Thomas, what have you been up to?" he shouted. "The Inspector is not pleased at all!"

Thomas felt terrible.

Thomas had to put things right.

He **heaved** and **hauled** Gordon to the Steamworks for repairs.

Soon, Gordon's funnel was fixed and his firebox was roaring again!

Thomas steamed back to the Docks.
He was ready to be a **very busy engine!**

He **shunted** and **shoved** until all the trucks
were in the right places.

He didn't see that The Fat Controller and the
Inspector were watching him!

"You've been a **very busy engine**," the Inspector said to Thomas.

"Next time, Thomas," said The Fat Controller, "remember that you can be a busy engine all by yourself and a Really Useful one, too."

And Thomas beamed from buffer to buffer!

PEEP! PEEP!

The End